LANCE ARMSTRONG

DISCOVER THE LIFE OF A SPORTS STAR

David and Patricia Armentrout

Rourke

Publishing LLC

Vero Beach, Florida 32964

© 2004 Rourke Publishing LLC

www.rourkepublishing.com

PHOTO CREDITS: All photos © Getty Images

Title page: *Lance speeds through the streets of Lorient, France, during a Tour de France time trial.*

Editor: Frank Sloan

Cover and interior design by Nicola Stratford

Library of Congress Cataloging-in-Publication Data

Armentrout, David, 1962-
  Lance Armstrong / David and Patricia Armentrout.
     v. cm. — (Discover the life of a sports star)
Includes bibliographical references and index.
Contents: American cyclist — Sports in Texas — Triathlete — An early career — World champion — The Tour DuPont — Tour de France success — Biggest race of his life — Four-time Tour de France winner — Dates to remember.
  ISBN 1-58952-651-1 (hardcover)
  1. Armstrong, Lance—Juvenile literature. 2. Cyclists—United States—Biography—Juvenile literature. [1. Armstrong, Lance. 2. Bicyclists. 3. Cancer—Patients.] I. Armentrout, Patricia, 1960- II. Title. II. Series: Armentrout, David, 1962- Discover the life of a sports star.
  GV1051.A76A75 2003
  796.6'2'092—dc21
                                                        2003005930

Printed in the USA

CG/CG

Table of Contents

Lance Armstrong is an American cycling champion.

American Cyclist

Lance Armstrong is a great American **cyclist**. In fact, he may be the best cyclist in the world. Being the best did not come easy for Lance. He got to the top by working hard and overcoming challenges.

Born: September 18, 1971 in Plano, Texas
Resides: Austin, Texas and Nice, France
Team: United States Postal Service
Record: Four-time Tour de France Champion
Sports Illustrated Sportsman of the Year 2002

Sports in Texas

Lance was always interested in sports. His favorite sports were those that involved racing. First, he joined a local swim team. He loved **competing**. He tried running next and joined his school's cross-country team. He also began racing bicycles.

Lance soon heard about a new sport called **triathlon**. The sport combines swimming, running, and cycling. Lance signed up for every race he could.

Racers prepare for the swimming leg of a triathlon.

Lance's mother is his biggest fan.

Triathlete

Lance lived with his mother. They often struggled to make ends meet. Lance's mother, however, was his biggest fan. Mrs. Armstrong did all she could to make sure Lance was able to race. Sometimes they had to drive for days to get to the next race. Lance worked hard and became one of the best **triathletes** in Texas.

Lance races in the 1996 Olympics.

An Early Career

One day a man asked Lance if he would join the USA Junior National Team. Lance was only 17, but it was the opportunity he had dreamed of. Soon, Lance was competing in international events.

In 1992, Lance entered his first **Olympic Games** competition. He came in 20th. He competed in his first **professional** race that same year. He finished last, but he knew he could do better.

Lance, wearing the rainbow-striped jersey, talks to American cycling star Greg LeMond.

World Champion

Many of the world's best bike racers live and train in Europe. Lance decided to move to Italy to train with the best. Long hours of training on steep roads in the mountains paid off. In 1993, Lance won the World Championship race in Norway. The cycling world was stunned that this newcomer had won this important race. As the winner, Lance won the right to wear the famous rainbow-striped jersey. This showed he was the world champion.

The Tour DuPont

The most important annual bike race in the United States is called the Tour DuPont. Lance had come in second in this race, but had never won. Lance and his team trained hard, and in 1995 they won the Tour DuPont. Lance was happy to win the big race in his own country.

Now it was time for Lance to set his sights on cycling's biggest event—the Tour de France.

Cyclists, including Lance, race along foggy mountain roads during the Tour DuPont.

Tour de France Success

Bikers dream of winning the Tour de France. The race is held in stages and takes three weeks to complete. Lance had raced in the Tour de France before, but had never finished. Lance finished the race and even won one of the stages. The 1995 race will always be a sad memory for Lance, however. His good friend and teammate, Fabio Casartelli, was killed when he crashed his bike in the mountains.

The Tour de France is more than 2,000 miles (3,200 km) long.

Lance's friend, comedian Robin Williams, rides in an event that raises money for Lance's foundation. The foundation supports cancer survivors.

Biggest Race of His Life

In the fall of 1996, Lance got some awful news. His doctors told him he had **cancer**. Lance had faced challenges before, but this one would take all his strength to overcome. Lance and his doctors came up with a plan to save his life.

After months of treatments that left him feeling terrible, Lance's doctors gave him the best news of his life. The cancer was gone. Lance had won the biggest race of his life.

Four-time Tour de France Winner

By late 1997, Lance was back. He joined the U.S. Postal Service team and started training. After winning a few races, Lance was ready to compete in the 1999 Tour de France. He not only competed, he won! He won again in 2000, 2001, and 2002.

Lance isn't finished yet. In fact, fitness tests show that he is stronger now than he was 10 years ago. He continues training and racing, and lives with his wife and three children in Texas.

Lance celebrates his 2002 Tour de France win with his family.

Dates to Remember

1971	Born in Texas
1992	Enters first Olympic competition
1993	Wins World Championship race in Norway
1995	Wins Tour DuPont
1996	Lance learns that he has cancer
1997	Doctors tell Lance his cancer is gone
1997	Joins U.S. Postal Service bike racing team
1998	Marries Kristin Richard
1999	Wins Tour de France
2000	Wins Tour de France
2001	Wins Tour de France
2002	Wins Tour de France

Glossary

cancer (KAN sur) — a disease in which some cells in the body grow faster than normal cells, destroying organs and tissue

competing (kum PEET ing) — striving to win a goal

cyclist (SYE klist) — a bicycle rider

Olympic Games (oh LIM pic GAYMZ) — a competition in summer and winter sports held every four years for athletes all over the world

professional (pruh FESH uh nuhl) — someone paid to participate in a sport

triathletes (trye ATH leetz) — athletes who compete in the triathlon

triathlon (trye ATH lon) — a long distance race that combines three sports

Index

Further Reading

Armstrong, Kristin. *Lance Armstrong: The Race of His Life*. Grosset and
    Dunlap, 2000.
Stewart, Mark. *Sweet Victory: Lance Armstrong's Incredible Journey*.
    The Millbrook Press, 2000.

Websites To Visit

www.lancearmstrong.com/
www.laf.org/
www.lancearmstrongfanclub.com/
www.tourdefrancenews.com/

About The Authors

David and Patricia Armentrout have written many nonfiction books for young readers.
They have had several books published for primary school reading. The Armentrouts
live in Cincinnati, Ohio, with their two children.